Winter Eyes

Winter Eyes

Poems & Paintings by **Douglas Florian**

Greenwillow Books, New York

Watercolor paints and colored pencils were used for the full-color art.
The text type is Schneidler.
Copyright © 1999 by Douglas Florian
All rights reserved. No part of this book may be reproduced or utilized
in any form or by any means, electronic or mechanical, including
photocopying, recording, or by any information storage and retrieval
system, without permission in writing from the Publisher,
Greenwillow Books, a division of William Morrow & Company, Inc.,
1350 Avenue of the Americas, New York, NY 10019.
Manufactured in China by South China Printing Company Ltd.
First Edition   10   9

Library of Congress Cataloging-in-Publication Data

Florian, Douglas.
Winter eyes / by Douglas Florian.
p.   cm.
Summary: A collection of poems about winter, including
"Sled," "Icicles," and "Ice Fishing."
ISBN 0-688-16458-7
1. Children's poetry, American.   2. Winter—Juvenile poetry.
[1. Winter—Poetry.   2. American poetry.]   I. Title.
PS3556.L589W56   1999   811'.54—dc21
98-19483   CIP   AC

For my mother,
Edith Florian

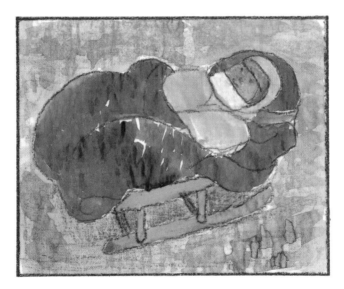

Contents

WINTER EYES

Look at winter
With winter eyes,
As smoke curls from rooftops
To clear cobalt skies.

Breathe in winter
Past winter nose:
The sweet scent of black birch
Where velvet moss grows.

Walk through winter
With winter feet
On crackling ice
Or sloshy wet sleet.

Listen to winter
With winter ears:
The rustling of oak leaves
As spring slowly nears.

What I Love About Winter

Frozen lakes
Hot pancakes
Lots of snow
Hot cocoa
Skates and skis
Evergreen trees
Funny hats
Thermostats
Sunsets blaze
Holidays
Snowball fights
Fireplace nights
Chimneys steaming
Winter dreaming

WHAT I HATE ABOUT WINTER

Frozen toes
Running nose
Sloppy slush
Holiday crush
15 below
Shoveling snow
Leafless trees
Cough and wheeze
Shorter day
Less time to play
Salt-spreading tractors
Windchill factors
No place to go—
Winter is slow

WINTER HUES

Winter has to pick and choose.
The clothes she wears
Are few in hues:
A raw sienna,
A dark burnt umber,
Some yellow ochres
Scant in number,
Steel gray day,
Navy night,
And winter white
And winter white.

Winter Songs

The winter sings a windy song
That hustles rusty leaves along.

The winter sings a song of hail
That pings and pangs like falling nails.

The winter sings a song of sleet
As sloshing cars slip down the street.

The winter sings a song of snow,
A whispering as
                  whiteness
                      grows.

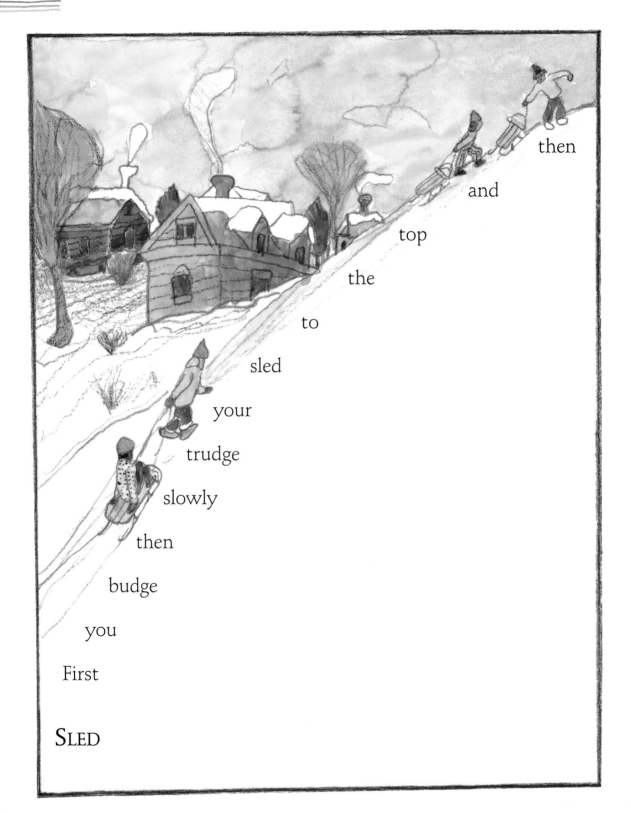

then

and

top

the

to

sled

your

trudge

slowly

then

budge

you

First

SLED

you
   s
     p
      e
       e
        d
       you
        s
         a
          i
           l
           you
             w
              h
               i
                z
                you
                  w
                   a
                    i
                     l
              and
           start
       all
     over
again.

THE WINTER SUN

The winter sun's a grumpy guy.
He scarcely gets to see the sky.
He doesn't speak. His rays are weak.
His disposition's grim and bleak.
He hovers near the naked trees,
His blanket from the sky's big freeze,
And barely dares to lift his head
Before he's ordered back to bed.

THE WINTER TREE

The winter tree
Is fast asleep.
She dreams, in reams
Of snow knee-deep,
Of children climbing
Up her trunk,
Of white-tailed deer
And gray chipmunk,
Of picnics,
Hammocks,
And short sleeves,
And leaves
    And leaves
        And leaves
            And leaves.

WINTER INSIDE

Winter is cold.
Winter is ice.
But winter inside
Is cozy and nice.

Winter is snow.
Winter is sleet.
But winter inside
Is fireplace feet.

Winter is bitter.
Winter is biting.
But winter inside
Is very inviting.

WINTER TRACKS

The meadow mouse is rarely seen
When earth is soft and leaves are green.
But on the freshly fallen snow
You'll spot the tracks that come and go,
The tracks that come and go until
Inside a cubbyhole they spill.

ICICLES

Icicles are winter's fingers
That form where freezing water lingers.

Icicles are winter's arrows
Pointing out the crows and sparrows.

Icicles are dragon's teeth.
They don't grow up.
They drip beneath.

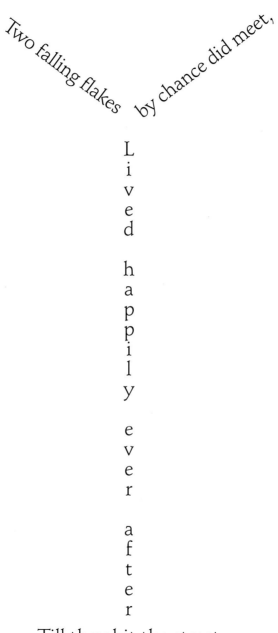

Two falling flakes by chance did meet,

L
i
v
e
d

h
a
p
p
i
l
y

e
v
e
r

a
f
t
e
r

Till they hit the street.

SNOW MAN, SNOW WOMAN

Snow man.
Snow woman.
They are not real.
They are not human.
They cannot walk,
They cannot creep,
Except when humans
Are asleep.

SUGARING TIME

When winter's thaw
Has just begun,
Then maple sap
Begins to run.
Up the tree
And out the spout
Into a bucket
The sap drips out.
Two horses haul it
From the grove
To where it's boiled
On a stove.
Then from a faucet
To a kettle.
The syrup quickly
Heats the metal.
But when it cools,
After a while,
You pour it on
Your pancake pile.
The work is done.
It's time to eat.
Sugaring time
Is surely sweet.

Winter Time

Summer hums.
It speeds along.

Spring zings,
A brief sweet song.

Autumn falls,
Thin as a dime.

But winter
    always
    takes
    its
    time.

CABIN FEVER

I've done the wash.
I've swept the floor.
I've fed the cat
And fixed the door.
I've read three books
And last week's news,
And for the fourth time
Polished shoes.
It seems like years
Since I've had fun.
I look outside
For signs of sun.
I bite my nails.
I crawl the walls.
For lack of space
I pace the halls.
My mother warned me
Of cabin fever.
I was a fool
To not believe her.

Winter Burrows

Beneath the pond a sleeping frog
Recalls she was a polliwog,
Once wiggling wild beside a log.

The rusty fox deep in his hole
Dreams of chasing mouse and mole,
Schemes of racing red-backed vole.

The fat-cheeked chipmunk can be found
Inside her burrow underground.
She dreams without a single sound.

And me, I'm burrowed in my bed
With cozy quilt above my head
And dreams of snowman, sleigh, and sled.

Winter Wear

The weasel wears a coat of white.
He always keeps it zippered tight.
It helps him weasel out of sight.

The snowshoe hare from head to toe
Wears white wherever she may go
To help her hide against the snow.

The snowy owl perched in a tree
On snowy days is hard to see.
I don't see him, but he sees me.

In our white coats we come to peek.
On winter wildlife we sneak.
We play a game of hide-and-seek.

WINTER GREENS

On winter days there's no excuse
To not enjoy a Norway spruce.
I pine to see a tall white pine,
Magnificent in rain or shine.
The aromatic balsam fir
Is fine as any conifer.
And please observe, the hemlock tree
Is graced with handsome symmetry.
Though temperatures are in the teens,
My eyes eat up these winter greens.

ICE FISHING

First carve a hole into the ice.
A chisel or a spud works nice.
Then load the line with tasty bait . . .
     And wait
        And wait
           And wait
              And wait.

THE WINTER FIELD

In wintertime
Our football field
Turns hard as stone—
It doesn't yield.
To catch or guard
A forward pass
Is harder on
The hardened grass.
The icy air
Makes fingers numb.
A speeding football
Stings your thumb.
But as across
The field we race,
Our hearts beat with
A faster pace.
And when we dodge
And drive and score,
Our bodies warm,
Our spirits soar.
This winter field
That bumps and stings
We wouldn't trade
For anything.

WINTER WOOL

Woolen socks
And woolen vest,
In woolen shirts
And skirts we're dressed.
Woolen sweaters,
Woolen caps—
The ones that have two woolen flaps.
Woolen gloves
And woolen coats
With woolen scarves
Around our throats.
Woolen here
And woolen there.
Our heads are growing
Woolen hair.

WINTER WOOD

The winter wood no longer grows.
It's stacked in cords.
It's packed in rows.
Its sap is sapped,
Its bark stripped free,
Its roots and leaves
Mere memory.
This wood that grew
By weeds and grasses
Grows less and less
As

     winter

          passes.

WINTER LIVES

The "dead" of winter—
Or so they say.
But winter lives
In her own way.
She leaves her tracks,
She shows us signs:
Not brilliant blooms,
But webs of lines.
Not sprout or splash,
But silver gray.
Winter lives
In her own way.

WINTER BLADES

No more summer blades of grass.
Now on blades of steel we pass.
Blades to g l i d e with greatest ease
Or carve out great geometries.
Blades for hockey.
Blades for speed.
Blades of steel to steal a lead,
To spin until our senses reel.
Winter blades are made of steel.

FIGURE 8

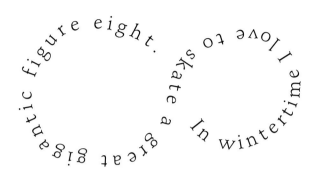

In wintertime I love to skate a great gigantic figure eight.

WINTER NIGHT

No summer haze.
No autumn mist.
The winter air
Is clean and crisp.
And when the moon
And stars appear,
They somehow seem
To be more near.
Orion shines,
Big Dipper's bright
Upon this wondrous
Winterous night.

GOOD-BYE, WINTER

Good-bye, winter.
Farewell.
Adieu.
We've really had
Enough of you.
Enough of frozen
Hands and toes.
Of numbing ears
And running nose.
Enough of sniffles,
Snivels, sneezes.
Enough of coughs
And whines and wheezes.
Enough of winter
Winds that sting.
Good-bye, winter.
Hello, spring!